# Tales from Acorn Wood

## Three lift-the-flap stories

# Julia Donaldson

# Axel Scheffler

MACMILLAN CHILDREN'S BOOKS

First published 2006 by Macmillan Children's Books
This edition published 2008 by Macmillan Children's Books
*Rabbit's Nap*, *Postman Bear* and *Hide-and-Seek Pig* first published 2000
by Macmillan Children's Books
a division of Macmillan Publishers Limited
20 New Wharf Road, London N1 9RR
Basingstoke and Oxford
Associated companies throughout the world
www.panmacmillan.com

ISBN: 978-1-4050-9025-4

Text copyright © Julia Donaldson 2000
Illustrations copyright © Axel Scheffler 2000, 2006
Moral rights asserted. All rights reserved.

5 7 9 8 6 4

A CIP catalogue record for this book is available from the British Library.

Printed in Malaysia

# Rabbit's Nap

Rabbit's feeling sleepy.
She curls up in a chair.

Tap! Tap! Who's that?
Oh dear! It's Builder Bear.

# Where can Rabbit have her nap?
The window seat looks nice.

Bang! Clash! Who's that?
Oh no! A band of mice.

Rabbit's in her deckchair.
A doze would be so good.

Whack! Crack! Who's that?
It's Fox – he's chopping wood.

"A shady tree!" says Rabbit.
"The kind of spot I like."

Ting-a-ling! Who's that?
It's Tortoise on his bike.

Poor tired Rabbit goes back home.
She yawns and rubs her eyes.

Rat-a-tat! Who's that?
"Your friends with a surprise!"

"Hush-a-bunny! Tra-la-la!
We'll sing you off to sleep!"

Zzzzz! Zzzzz! What's that?
Shall we have a peep?

# Postman Bear

# Bear is writing letters.
## One, two, three.

Bear goes out to post them.
Who lives in this tree?

# Shall we count the letters?

Only two.

Someone's home is in this pond.
Let's find out who.

Just one letter left now.
Who's it for?

Someone's made a heap of earth.

Who's behind this door?

# What was in those letters, One, two, three?

Would you like to open one?

Have a look and see.

Bear is in the kitchen.
Watch him cook.

# What's inside the oven?

Let's have a look.

Someone's knocking at the door.
One, two, three.

Bear goes to open it.
Who can it be?

"Happy Birthday, Bear!"

# Hide-and-Seek Pig

"Let's play hide and seek," says Hen.
"Yes," says Pig. "I'll count to ten."

Now it's time for Pig to seek.
Can you see a yellow beak?

"Come on, Blackbird, follow me.
Let's find Hen. Where can she be?"

Look! A tent! Is Hen in here?
Can you see a long brown ear?

"Come on, Rabbit, follow me.
Let's find Hen. Where can she be?"

Pig has found a spotty sheet.
Can you see a pair of feet?

"Come on, Squirrel, follow me. Let's find Hen. Where can she be?"

Maybe Hen's behind this pail.
Can you see a furry tail?

"Come on, Dormouse, follow me.
Let's find Hen. Where can she be?"

Who's behind this garden rose?
Can you see a stripy nose?

"Come on, Badger, follow me.
I'll lead you to our picnic tea."

Still no Hen! Where did she go?
Pig can't think. But do you know?